CONTEN

I would like to dedicate this book to Tony Eveleigh who was a great supporter of Nottingham Forest.

CHAPTER ONE

NOTHING CAN STOP US

"It's a goal!" Jamie shouted, jumping from his seat. The crowd roared and cheered, "Come on you Reds!"

The final whistle blew and the players began their lap of honour, saluting the fans with waves of victory.

"Grandad, we've won! Did you see it? What a goal!"

"Well, you certainly scored a goal right in my lap."

"Sorry," Jamie pulled a tissue from his pocket and dabbed at the puddle of tomato soup on his Grandad's knee.

"I'll do it. No harm done. At least it wasn't hot. Here I'll use this."

"But you'll spoil your Nottingham Forest hat," said Jamie.

"It's red anyway. There, that's it". Jamie's Grandad shook the hat and pushed the cup into his bag.

"Grandad, can we come next week?"

"I think there's no choice in the matter. We've got to come next week. We'll be playing for promotion."

"And we're going to the top!" shouted a young supporter from the seat below.

"Are we going to the top, Grandad?" asked Jamie. "Will we be in the Premiere League?"

"I think we can do it. With a team like this, nothing can stop us. It'll be like waving a magic wand. All they need to do is walk out on that pitch next week and we'll cheer them to victory."

"Victory, victory!" Jamie chanted.

"That's on Thursday. Come on, we need to buy our tickets for the game now. Let's get going. I want to get a good seat. And I'd better buy you some Velcro so I can stick you down. I don't want another lapful of tomato soup."

"How did it go?" Jamie's Dad was at the door to the house.

"Like a dream," said Grandad. "Like a dream."

"We won two nil!" shouted Jamie. "Danny scored both goals! The opposition didn't stand a chance. He was like a whirlwind. Nobody could stop him!"

"He's enjoyed it." Jamie's Grandad ruffled his hair. "A good match. Danny Lacey, the new striker, did very well. He's been a good signing. He'll be a key player in Thursday night's match."

"Can I go on Thursday, Dad?" Jamie pleaded.

"Two matches in one week? That's a bit expensive."

"I'll treat him," said Jamie's Grandad, as he climbed back into his car. "Say it's an early birthday present. He can't go missing the most important match of the season. I'll pick you up on Thursday, Jamie, and don't bring tomato soup!"

Jamie laughed and waved as the car drew away from the kerb. He watched it disappear into the distance, the Nottingham Forest scarf flying from the window.

CHAPTER TWO

MEET LEGENDWORLD.CO.UK

"We won!" Jamie ran into the school playground and grabbed Louise's arm. "We won on Saturday!"

"What was the score?"

"Two - nil, it was a great game. Two goals in the second half!"

"Jamie, can we forget about Saturday, please." Miss Foster appeared at the classroom door. "Today is Monday. I think you can save the football commentary for playtime. It's time to go in now. I want you all in quickly so that we can go down to the computer room."

"Are we going on the Internet?" Jack rushed to the door to be first in the queue.

"If you can all manage to walk down the corridor in a civilised fashion," said Miss Foster.

After registration the class lined up at the door, ready to file down the corridor. "Don't run," Louise whispered to Caroline. "If you do we'll have to go back to the classroom."

The journey complete, the class quietly took up their positions at the computer screens.

"I'd like you to log on then go on to the Internet," said Miss Foster.

"Can we go to a football website?" asked Kevin.

"You can do that at home," said Miss Foster, "This morning we're visiting a new site. It's linked to a series of children's books. You can start typing in the website address from the board, or put your hand up if you have difficulties. Read it out to me please, Jamie."

Jamie read the words on the white-board, "legendworld.co.uk"

"Hey, this looks good," said Louise, as a castle appeared on the computer screen, floating in a dark sky, and a pumpkin glowed in one window. She read the words on the screen aloud, "A World of Fairy Tale and Fantasy, Click on the door to enter." Louise clicked the mouse.

"There's a walking dragon," said Jamie when the image on the screen changed.

"Now, once you're on the site take a look around," said Miss Foster. "Be sure to read the latest news".

"Dragon, trolls. Let's look at Lost Dragons." Louise clicked on the box. "Look there's pictures of funny dragons – Dective!" Louise scrolled down the page. "Wilber!" She laughed out loud at the picture of the overweight dragon.

"Now, if you go to Lost Dragons," said Miss Foster, "you'll find out how to return dragons to Legendworld – very important."

Active fingers clicked. The information appeared on the screen.

"It says if you want to return a dragon to Legendworld you simply take a photo of it and email the photo to the website," said Miss Foster.

"Why would you want to send a dragon?" asked Sylvie. "They don't exist. It's silly. I've never seen a dragon in Nottingham. Dragons are only in Fairy Stories."

"This website carries extracts from stories about trolls, dragons and mythical creatures," Miss Foster explained. "It's a world of fairytale and fantasy, like it says on the first page. Now, if you go to the page called Latest News you'll find lots of pictures of dragons that children have sent in. You could send a picture to the website and have it displayed. You could even send one of your own stories."

"Miss Foster, I've lost the picture of the trolls," Sarah called out. Miss Foster went to her aid, leaving the class to explore the website.

"I hope we get to write stories about dragon catching," said Louise. "I'd find a dragon in my wardrobe and feed it on cornflakes. It would grow bigger and bigger, then I wouldn't be able to get in my bed."

"That's silly," said Tim. "The flames would scorch your duvet and the house would be on fire."

"It's my story," said Louise. "I can make anything happen in my story."

"Ideas then, let's get some ideas for stories," said Miss Foster, returning to the whole class.

"The Dragon in the Wardrobe," said Louise.

"Toasted Castle," shouted Tim.

"Dragon Plays for Nottingham Forest," said Anthea.

"The pitch is scorched by a torrent of flames – Manager says this player will…" shouted Tim.

"A little less noise please, Tim," said Miss Foster. "Now, let's get down some starter ideas before we leave the computer suite." She began to circulate amongst the children.

"Have you got any ideas Jamie?" she peered over his shoulder at the blank page. "I'm sure you can think of something." She ruffled his hair.

" I've got one," Nicholas called out. "Darin was in trouble. He'd robbed a bank and the police were after him. He wanted to hide so he emailed himself to Legendworld."

Miss Foster laughed. "Now that is using your imagination - emailing people to Legendworld. A good job it's only a fantasy idea. If it really worked I'd be emailing a few people to Legendworld." She looked round the room.

"Miss Foster!" Josh shot up his hand. "Can someone email me to Legendworld?"

"I'm only joking, Josh. You can't email people across the Internet."

"Miss Foster," Marie asked politely. "Why aren't there any pictures of people on the website?"

"Well.." Miss Foster began.

"You could have pictures of football players!" Tim called out. "That would be worth looking at."

"As I was beginning to say," Miss Foster took control again. "The stories on the website are about fairytale creatures so that's why the pictures are of dragons and trolls."

"Why aren't there any football stories?" Tim called out.

"Tim, if you want to write a story about football no one will stop you," said Miss Foster.

"And send it to Legendworld?" asked Tim.

"Well, no one can stop you emailing any story or picture to Legendworld but they might not publish it on the website."

"I'm going to try," said Tim.

"You do that," said Miss Foster. "Now, let's get some stories going."

"He won't do it," Louise whispered to Jamie. "When he gets home he'll rush out to play football and forget all about it."

"Miss Foster." Marie put her hand up again. "If you could email people to Legendworld how would you get them back?"

"I wouldn't want you to come back," said Daniel.

"All right, that's quite enough," said Miss Foster. "Exciting though it may be, I want to see you all working before lunch or I may be tempted to put the emailing to the test."

CHAPTER THREE

DISCOVERING THE CAVES

"Good morning. Can I help you?" The woman at the Nottingham Forest Football Club reception desk called over to the young man in the brightly coloured tee shirt.

"I'm looking for Danny Lacey. I've got a parcel for him."

"I can take it for him." The receptionist reached over the counter.

"I'd like to give it to him myself," said the young man.

"I'm afraid you won't be able to do that at the moment. He went out about an hour ago. I don't expect him back for a couple of hours. I think he's gone on a tour of Nottingham. If you leave it with me I'll make sure he gets it."

"I think I'll try again later." The man turned for the door.

"You could be unlucky," the receptionist called after him. "They've got a training session this afternoon. As soon as he comes back he'll be in the changing room."

Danny leant against the stone statue. Sadie had said 'Meet at the Lions.' He looked across the square at the other lion statue outside the Town Hall, a pair of lions. "Why lions in Nottingham?" Danny thought to himself. "Why not Robin Hood?"

"Danny! Danny!" a young woman's voice called from behind him. He turned round to see Sadie smiling.

"You haven't changed at all," she said. "You look just like you did at school."

"I'm a bit older than when we last met," said Danny.

"And you're a Nottingham Forest First Team player. Watch out, everybody will be asking you for your autograph."

"You're looking well," said Danny, taking Sadie's arm and walking away from the statue.

"Must be all the good food I'm eating. Or maybe it's because I'm enjoying myself at University," said Sadie.

"Always said you had a brain," Danny joked. "Well, where to? What's this tour of Nottingham you're taking me on?"

"We won't have time to see everything today. I thought we'd start with the caves. The entrance is in one of the shopping centres."

"Caves in a shopping centre? This should be interesting. Lead the way."

"Doesn't look very cave like. That's an umbrella canopy," said Danny, as they approached the cave entrance.

"What do you expect - a hole in the wall? We're in the middle of the Broad Marsh Shopping Centre. Come on, you'll need to get your pennies out." They went into the well-lit entrance. An assistant looked up from the desk.

"Two please," said Sadie.

"Would you like the audio commentary wands?" the young woman held out a broad red plastic wand covered in numbers, rather like a huge mobile phone.

"What are they for?" asked Danny.

"They tell you about each section in the caves," said the young woman. "Just press number one for the first section. Then press play. You have your own personal commentary."

"Oh, that's clever," said Sadie. "Yes, we'll have one each please."

"It's worth it," said the assistant. "And of course, you'll have to wear the hard hats."

"This is getting a bit scary," Sadie laughed. "Like going into a mine shaft."

"Are there rock falls?" asked Danny.

"No." The young woman laughed. "There are some low arches. You could bang your head on them. How's this for size?" She held out a red hat.

"The right colour for you," said Sadie, "Nottingham Forest colours."

"Try this," said the girl, pulling a red hat from the stand and offering it to Sadie.

"A bit on the large size," said Sadie.

"No more red. How about white?" asked the young woman. "I'm afraid we've got a school party in, so there's not so many small ones. Is that comfortable?"

"Fine," said Sadie, adjusting the white helmet. "Right, we're ready to go."

"Don't you want paying?" asked Danny.

"Oh, yes!" The young assistant laughed, a little embarrassed.

"It's your celebrity personality. She's overcome," said Sadie.

"Me?" Danny looked puzzled.

"Well, you've had your photo in 'The Evening Post' enough times in the last fortnight. You recognise him, don't you?" Sadie asked the young woman. The young woman nodded and smiled shyly.

"See. I told you," said Sadie. "You are a celebrity."

"Come on," said Danny. "We'd better start this tour. If I don't get back to the ground for training I won't even be in the team."

"This way." Sadie led Danny into a tunnel. "This rocks crumbling." She rubbed the wall of the cave with her finger.

"It's sandstone," said Danny. "It's very light in here. Imagine what it was like eight hundred years ago. It would have been pitch black and lit by candles when it was first burrowed out."

"Right, this is section one," said Sadie. "We press one on this device and we'll hear all about it." She pressed the key and held the audio wand to her ear. "I can't hear anything. Can you hear anything?"

"It's talking about the Second World War and the time the caves were used as air-raid shelters," said Danny.

"Well, it's saying nothing to me," said Sadie. "Press one, then play." She tried again. "Nothing. It's still not working. I give up. Just tell me what's happening. I'll stay close to you."

"Come on then," said Danny. "Looks like I'm leading the tour. Follow me."

"Where are we now?" asked Sadie.

"Section Eight," said Danny, holding the audio wand to his ear. "This is the Tannery."

"Are those animal skins? " asked Sadie.

"Yes. This is where they turned them into leather. See all those holes and troughs filled with water cut into the bottom of the cave?"

"Yes."

"Some were filled with dog dung and urine to clean the lime off the skins after they'd been soaked."

"Ugh, sounds awful," said Sadie. "You wouldn't get my hands in there without rubber gloves."

Danny laughed. "They hadn't invented rubber gloves two hundred years ago."

"Let's move on," said Sadie. She keyed in another number. "It's no good. I think I've got a faulty one. I can't hear anything. I'll take it back."

"Now?"

"Yes, I won't be long. You can go and look at the next section. I'll catch up with you when I get back." Sadie turned to go. "Just a minute, what's up here?" She walked down a narrow passageway. "Come and see what this is about." She beckoned Danny to follow her.

Sadie stopped at a tall iron-railed gate. "There's no number on it, but it must be something to do with the caves. Probably a new section."

Danny peered through the iron bars into the darkness of the cave. "There's a monk in there."

"Spooky," said Sadie, looking at the dark, hooded figure. "I bet it's supposed to be the ghostly Brother Benedict – the monk who walks the caverns."

"Brother Benedict, the ghost? Now that has to be make believe," said Danny.

"It's up to you if you believe it, but he was seen."

15

"A monk!"

"The ghost of a monk," said Sadie.

"Who parades around every night?"

"Well, maybe not every night, but he's been seen once, so far. It was in the 1960's, when they first decided to close off the caves. Before this shopping centre was built some archaeologists were researching the site and one of them saw this apparition – a brown monk walking through a cave wall, straight through. One minute he was there. The next he disappeared."

"Sounds like anyone could have made that up," said Danny.

"Well, I told you, believe it or not. But just be very careful whilst I'm gone. Mind Brother Benedict, there, doesn't get you. Don't go far, I'm just going to get a new listening device. I'll be back in a minute." Sadie went back along the pathway.

Danny looked again for a number on the wall. Nothing. He peered through the railings. The light in the caves beyond was dimmed. He could just pick out the cowl-hooded figure of the monk. He tried to open the gate but it was locked. "Probably for security," he thought to himself. Then he looked at his watch. "I hope Sadie's not long. I have to be back in time for the training session. Bet she's at least ten minutes."

He turned round and leant his back against the metal gate, folding his arms and waiting. There was a slight movement, and then suddenly the gate swung open. Danny almost overbalanced, grabbing one of the railings to stop himself from falling backwards.

Once he'd steadied himself again he took a step into the cave. There was no artificial light. The walls had lost their gold, sandstone lustre in the darkness. He peered around into one of the burrowed out chambers and brushed against the monk's shoulder. It felt so life-like that Danny had to step back and take a closer look at the motionless figure. He wondered what it was made from. Wax? The deep hood completely covered the profile of the face.

Perhaps he'd take a look underneath. He touched the fabric, gently lifting the edge. As he did so the gate behind him slammed closed. Danny jumped at the noise then turned to see the gate-bolt slide into place. A hand came across his face and another curled around his chest. He found himself being dragged backwards across the cave floor. He tried to shout out but the hand clamped tighter as he was pulled further into the darkness.

"Press and play." Sadie engaged the new device, lifting it to her ear.

"Is it okay?" asked the young assistant at the desk.

"Fine, I think it's fine."

"Good, have fun."

"Thank you." Sadie began her journey back into the cave system, in search of Danny.

"Danny, I've got a new one." Sadie walked towards the metal grilled door. "It's a lot better. Danny!" But he was nowhere to be seen.

She turned back along the pathway, thinking that he'd gone on ahead without her. In one section some school children were playing the old pub games, knocking over skittles and trying to 'Catch the rat'. Sadie moved between them. "Have you seen a young man pass?" she asked the teacher.

"Don't know, I've got to keep all of my eyes on these."

"Oh, thank you anyway," and Sadie moved on. At the exit she hung up her helmet and turned to one of the assistants. "You haven't seen a young man come through here on his own in the last fifteen minutes have you?"

"I really wouldn't remember," said the girl. "We've had quite a few visitors this morning, including a party of school children. I'm sorry."

"Could he have got lost in the caves or got out another way?" asked Sadie.

"This is the only way out. No, everyone comes through this way. He's probably gone. But I just can't remember. Have you got a mobile phone? If he comes back I could get him to call you. Do you want to leave a message?"

"No, thank you," said Sadie, putting down her audio wand.

"Well, I hope you find him again." The assistant smiled. "I could leave a note at the desk to say where you'll be."

"No, don't bother. I think my sight seeing tour of Nottingham has come to an end."

CHAPTER FOUR

THE FRIAR TRAP

"Right, are you all listening? Where's Danny?" The Nottingham Forest Team Coach looked round the changing room. "I said everybody here and ready by 2 o'clock and it's 2.15!"

"Probably got his head stuck in a book somewhere," said one player.

"Said he was going to town this morning to meet a friend," another player called out.

"No, he's on a flight to Barbados. Didn't he win the roll-over on the lottery?" shouted another player.

"Could be watching the kit go round in the washing machine. I'll go to the Laundry Room." One of the players jumped up from the bench.

"No you don't, stay here! I don't want to lose another player. He'll have to have a very good excuse when I meet him. Right, you lot, let's get on that pitch!"

Danny pulled himself up from the floor, rubbing his eyes and adjusting his vision. Across the cave he could see the crouched figure of the monk, his face illuminated by a bright screen. Danny looked in amazement. The Monk was using a laptop computer.

"Are you all right?" The monk pulled down his hood and turned round to face Danny. Danny just stared at the baldhead surrounded by a fringe of grey hair.

"I suppose you'll be getting hungry. I feel peckish myself." The monk rubbed his fat stomach. "I shall have to go in search of food."

"What am I doing here?" asked Danny. "You've no right to keep me here!"

"Be patient. I just need to finish off this writing." The monk continued typing on the computer.

"I want to leave right now!" said Danny.

"Patience was never one of your virtues. I thought you would grow more patient as you grew older," said the monk, turning from the screen. "Now please let me finish."

"I want an explanation, now!" shouted Danny.

"Robin, I'm here, your trusted servant and guide. Why do you doubt me?" The figure began to stand. Holding the computer at waist height to light his path, he walked towards Danny. "The light in here is so poor. Praise the Lord that this screen denotes light."

"I'm not Robin. You've got the wrong person!" Danny edged away from the approaching figure. "Don't come any closer!"

"Robin, why are you so vexed? It is I, your friend. Look." He held the computer screen up to his face.   The broad, chubby features of an elderly, balding man were highlighted in the darkness. "Surely, you recognise me. That potion must have been strong to so blight your memory."

"I don't know you. Stay back! How do I get out of here?" Danny ran to the gate.

"Robin, stay!" The monk reached out his hand and grasped Danny's arm.

"Let go!" Danny shouted, pulling away. "Get off me! Who are you, dressed up like a monk?"

"It is I, your dear friend, Friar Tuck. Robin, don't play jokes. Please be yourself. You cannot fool an old friend. Your clothes may be different. But I know you are Robin Hood."

"I am not Robin Hood! My name's Danny! Now just let me out of here!"

"No, I want to get you safely back to the Medieval time layer. You cannot stay here. Today is Monday and the Annual Archery Tournament is on Friday morning. All your friends are most upset that you have chosen to go Time Travelling again at this important time."

"You are not talking sense." Danny grabbed at the computer. "Give me that. I'll find my way out. I'll email Nottingham Forest Football Club!"

"You must return to the forest. I'm not letting you go now that I've found you again." The Friar clung to the laptop and the two figures jostled in the darkness, the screen's light flashing on faces, shoulders and the walls of the cave.

"Don't be ridiculous, Robin! Come to your senses," shouted the Friar.

"I have come to my senses. Give it to me now. I'm going!" Danny swung round, yanking the computer clear out of the Friar's hands.

"Robin, you are not yourself!" The Friar dived to grab Danny's ankles before he could take his next step.

"Get off, you fool, get off!" Danny toppled to the floor, the computer shooting out before him. Its screen illuminating the ceiling of the cave.

"You must stay. I will use all the force I can muster," shouted the Friar. Danny felt the full weight of the Friar's bulk as he sat on his back. "I have made a great effort to be here and I have borrowed some equipment from Legendworld which must be returned before people notice I have it. Just relax. All will be well."

"Get off," Danny's muffled voice came from below.

"I regret that is your wish but I am doing this for the good of all. I have one of those devices called a digital camera in the Legendworld bag. Tomorrow I will take our photos then email them to Legendworld and we will both be returned safely to Medieval Nottingham again, in time for the tournament on Friday."

"I've got a football match for Nottingham Forest on Thursday night! You can't keep me here! It's kidnapping. You're insane!" Danny shouted.

The Friar laughed. "Now that sounds like the old Robin. Soon you'll be saying I'm a fat, gluttonous Friar."

"Get off, you elephant! Gorilla!" Danny's shouts echoed round the cave, as did the Friar's laughter.

"How's it going then? Have you had a good training session?" Nottingham Forest's Manager called to the coach from down the corridor, as mud-laden players ran into the changing room.

"Okay. We're getting there," said the coach.

"Thursday's an important match. We need to be saying better than that."

"If the whole squad came to train, I'd be saying it's 'in the bag'. Hey, I'm not a turnstile!" The coach was jostled as two players ran by.

"Sorry coach!" they called as they ran into the changing room.

"Who's missing?" asked the Manager.

"Danny."

"Where is he then?"

"You tell me," said the coach. "Gone for a walk-about. Good signing he may be, but if he doesn't train with the team we won't have a team.

Football is not about one player. It's building up a squad that can play together."

"Has he phoned in?" The Manager looked concerned.

"I've heard nothing."

"He's watching the washing!" a player called from the changing room.

"Great detectives in there," said the coach.

"Let me know as soon as you hear anything," said the Manager. "This isn't like Danny to just not turn up. There must be a good reason."

CHAPTER FIVE

THROUGH TIME AND SPACE

"Are you coming down for tea?" Jamie's Dad called from the bottom of the stairs.

"In a minute. I'm just finishing something," Jamie called back.

"Well, don't be long. This food will be ready in five minutes."

Jamie laid the magazine face down on the scanner bed. Then closed the lid and started the scan. The machine whirred.

The image of Danny slowly appeared on the computer screen. Jamie checked it out. It looked good. In fact it was one of his best photos of Danny heading the ball into the net. He saved the picture and prepared to send it as an attachment. He'd written down the email address: *returns@legendworld.co.uk.*

He pressed send. Done. Jamie sat back in the chair. Tim would be surprised when he saw Danny on the Legendworld website in the morning. But Jamie couldn't be sure that Legendworld had received the picture. He decided not to tell anyone until he was sure the email had arrived at its destination. He would check after tea.

"You've been a long time up there." Jamie's Dad turned from the grill as Jamie walked into the kitchen. "Have you been glued to that computer again?"

"I was just emailing something. What's for tea?"

"Sausages."

"I hope they're not herby sausages."

"No, I've bought these special tasteless sausages just for you." His Dad pulled the grill pan out. "This isn't my choice."

"They look good," said Jamie.

"Well, I hope they taste good to you. I'll be having a lot of sauce on mine." His Dad tipped sausages onto Jamie's plate.

"What's happening at school, then?"

"Oh, nothing. Same as usual," said Jamie.

"Your days must be boring if nothing happens." His Dad sat down at the table with his food.

"My football magazine didn't come today," said Jamie, slicing through a sausage.

"That's all that's on your mind, football."

"Can you phone up and ask why they didn't deliver it?"

"A please might help."

"Please."

"I'll try tomorrow lunch time."

"Maybe they delivered it next door," said Jamie.

"I think someone would have brought it round."

"They'll be reading it, first," said Jamie.

His Dad laughed. "You're becoming very suspicious of people in your old age."

"Well, I bet Robert will read it."

"You don't even know that they've got the magazine next door. If you're so convinced why don't you go round and ask for it?"

"I've got to do something first." Jamie pushed back his plate and got up from the table.

"And where are you going so quickly? Don't you want any pudding?"

"No thanks, I'm full," said Jamie.

"If you're going back to that computer you'd better not forget I want you to help with the washing up tonight."

"I will," said Jamie. "I just want to check something out." He opened the door into the hall and ran upstairs.

At the computer Jamie looked at his recent email messages. Yes, there was one from Legendworld. They must have received the photo and were thanking him. He brought up the message on the screen.

'Legendworld would like to thank you for Danny Lacey from Nottingham Forest Football Club.'

He'd done it! He wouldn't tell anyone until he checked out the website in the morning. There'd probably be a picture of Danny on the Legendworld notice board. That would surprise everyone at school.

CHAPTER SIX

EATING OUT IN NOTTINGHAM

The morning light crept into the cave. The Friar grunted in his sleep and tried to turn over on the hard floor. He looked up at the ceiling and remembered where he was. "Robin, have you slept well?" he called out, lifting his bulk from the cavern floor. "I expect you are stiff, like me. I wish I'd brought a feather mattress." He laughed, pulled his rope-belt tighter round his waist and called out again. "Robin, are you still asleep? Don't play games."

There was no reply from the crumpled blanket in the corner. The Friar shuffled over and lifted the edge of the blanket. "Trickery!" He looked down at the bare floor. "This is trickery, indeed, to escape when I'm asleep."

He plodded over to the closed door. "Locked!" He pushed on the metal bars. "Robin must have a Legendworld bracelet too. I shall find you, Robin, have no fear."

Jamie was eager to get to school that morning. He wanted to share his triumph. Tim would be jealous.

"Don't forget your lunchbox. You're in a hurry." His Dad passed him the box through the car window. "I'll see you tonight. I'm home early."

"Okay," Jamie gave a brief wave then sped off into the school playground. Louise was standing at the wall. Jamie called out to her, "I sent a photo of Danny to Legendworld last night, and I got a message back!"

"What did it say?"

"Something about 'thank you for sending Danny Lacey'."

"You didn't send Danny," said Louise.

"No!" Jamie laughed. "I sent a photo. I hope we go on the website again today. Everyone will see the photo of Danny."

"We won't get on the Internet today," said Louise. "Miss Foster's away."

"Umm." The Friar's nostrils were filled with an aroma of freshly grilled, sizzling bacon. He followed his nose round the corner. "Umm." He patted his fat stomach. "I am indeed hungry and that smell is most agreeable." He peered into the restaurant. A man got up from the table and went through a door. The waitress approached the table carrying a plate filled with bacon, eggs, beans and slices of toast. She put the plate on the man's table and went back to the counter.

The Friar looked round. No one else was about. There was no rush to find Robin. It was only Tuesday. He had until Thursday night to accomplish his mission. Now hunger called. The waitress's back was turned. He just couldn't resist the temptation.

CHAPTER SEVEN

THE MESSAGE FROM LEGENDWORLD

Jamie threw his coat down on the floor in the hallway of his house. Louise had been right. Miss Foster was away all day and they didn't use the computers. He would have to check the website at home.

"Jamie, hang your coat up when you come home from school, and don't drop your bag on the floor," his Dad called out from the kitchen as Jamie raced up the stairs.

Jamie ignored the request. He needed to see if Danny was on the website. Once in the spare room, he activated the computer. Would there be a photo of Danny? He found the website and went straight to the Notice Board - Dragons, more dragons! He scrolled down. It was there - the photo of Danny. Jamie ran to the top of the stairs. "Dad, I've emailed a photo of Danny to Legendworld!"

"I don't care if you've emailed last night's dinner. I want you to clear up these things now or you won't be going out for the rest of the week!"

Jamie dried the last cup in the kitchen, hung up the tea towel and went to join his Dad in the lounge.

"Dad, why do you use so many pans when you cook tea? There was a lot of washing up."

"Well, you could do with the practice." His Dad laughed. "Come and watch the News. There's something about Nottingham Forest."

"Today the police joined in the investigation into the disappearance of young First team footballer, Danny Lacey. The team Manager is very concerned. There has been no contact with him since yesterday morning. Family members think he may have been kidnapped as an act of sabotage before the big-match."

"They can't keep Danny! Dad, if Danny doesn't come back we won't win on Thursday!"

"They'll substitute."

"That's no good. Danny's a key player!"

"If he's not back that's all they can do," said Jamie's Dad.

"We've got to win on Thursday!"

"I'm sure they'll find him before Thursday." Jamie's Dad stood up from the settee. "Watch some cartoons. They'll cheer you up." He changed channels with the remote control. "I'll just check the fridge. See what we've got for sandwiches tomorrow. Keep the seat warm for me."

Jamie pulled his knees up onto the settee. The cartoon characters darted around the screen. But Jamie was not watching. His mind was on other things. Where was Danny? If he'd been kidnapped

34

someone would have to pay the ransom. They could have a collection in every school in Nottingham. But it could take days to get the money, even weeks. Why did they have to take Danny? But no one had sent a ransom note. Kidnappers always sent ransom notes. Maybe he hadn't been kidnapped.

Maybe…His mind began to race. No, that was stupid. How could he begin to think that? Miss Foster had said you couldn't email real people to Legendworld. It was all make believe. No, he'd only emailed a photo of Danny to Legendworld. You couldn't send a real person across the Internet.

"All made and packed." Jamie's Dad came back into the lounge as Jamie jumped up from the settee. "Where are you running off to?"

"I just want to check something on the computer," said Jamie, heading for the door.

"Three minutes that's all," his Dad called after him. "Don't spend all night up there."

Jamie bounded up the stairs. Was it possible? He sat at the computer, his mind filled with thoughts of Danny. "No, Danny's not in Legendworld. It can't happen. You can't email a person across the Internet, can you? But you never know…" He gazed at the computer screen then logged into his email account and began to type in a message.

Would you please send back….

When the message was complete Jamie sat back in the chair. Legendworld would think he was crazy asking for Danny back. But they'd probably just send back the photo. He pressed send. There he'd done it. Now he could forget all about the Legendworld emailing.

"Jamie are you staying up there all night?" his Dad called from downstairs.

"I'll be down in a minute." Jamie prepared to close down the computer for the night. But something flashed on the screen. He had a new email. It was from Legendworld.

"A message from Legendworld." His brain began to race. "What do they want? Maybe they didn't understand. Maybe they thought I was being silly, asking for a person to be returned." He brought the new message up on the screen.

Jamie, you seem to be causing confusion with your emails – I think it's time to come and see you myself.
Dierling.

Dierling! Who or what was Dierling? Jamie was not going to wait in the darkened bedroom long enough to find out.

CHAPTER EIGHT

DIERLING

"Well, I am honoured. That was quick. I didn't expect you down from the computer so soon." Jamie's Dad turned from the kitchen cupboard as Jamie raced into the kitchen. "Do you want a drink before you go to bed?"

"Yes, I'll put the kettle on," said Jamie, going to the work surface.

"Only enough for two cups. We're not having a bath in it," his Dad called out as the water sprayed from the tap. "Are you concentrating on what you're doing?"

Jamie didn't hear. Something caught his eye in the garden. The shed door was ajar, swinging in the wind.

"Jamie, turn it off!" his Dad leant over and tightened the gushing tap. "You'll have a flood in here!"

Jamie could see the shed door begin to open. A black shape emerged. He held his breath.

"Jamie, are we having a drink now or at Christmas? That cat, it's always sleeping in our shed. I'll have to fix that door."

"It's just a cat," said Jamie.

"What did you think it was?" his Dad asked. "A monster from the deep? Come on, you make the tea. I'll go out and fix the shed."

Jamie lingered in the doorway. He could see his Dad in the garden. The kitchen door at the other side of the room suddenly slammed to with the draught. Jamie ran into the garden.

"You don't need to come. I thought you were making the tea?" His Dad looked surprised when Jamie joined him at the shed door.

"It's okay, I'll watch," said Jamie, turning to see the well-lit kitchen beckoning. But he preferred to stay with his Dad in the darkness of the garden.

"Come on then. You can help hold this torch while I use the screwdriver." His Dad reached into his tool bag. "I think I need a new one, but it will have to wait. There, that will hold it." He screwed the screw in firmly. "Done. Let's go get that cup of tea."

Jamie stayed close to his Dad as they made their way back to the kitchen.

"Hey, it's a bit steamy in here! Jamie, you didn't put the lid back on the kettle properly."

Jamie ran to switch off the kettle.

"We'd better leave the door open to let out the steam," said his Dad.

"No! No!" said Jamie, reaching up to the small top window. "I'll open the window."

"It's like a fog in here." His Dad went to open the door.

"It'll be all right," said Jamie. "I'll open another top window."

"We'll see." His Dad closed the door again. "But if the steam doesn't clear soon I'll have to open the door and risk Mrs. Bootle's cat coming in. Right let's get this tea."

"Shame about Danny," said Jamie's Dad, as he set his empty cup on the kitchen table. "It's a mystery where he's gone. No-one seems to be safe nowadays."

"Dad, can we play a game tonight?"

"A game? I thought you'd be wanting to rush back upstairs to play games on the computer. I don't know if I've got the energy to play board-games."

"Go on, Dad, please," Jamie pleaded. "You're always saying we never do enough things together."

"Okay, I'm won over. You go choose a game upstairs. I'll just pour another cup of tea and go through to the lounge."

"This one's all right," Jamie pulled a box from a chair.

"That's old. You've got better games upstairs."

"I want to play this," Jamie insisted.

"It's your choice." His Dad began to pour out another cup of tea. "You go through and set it up."

"It's all right, I'll wait for you."

"Well, it looks like I win. I would be a millionaire if I really owned all this property." Jamie's Dad tapped the cards in front of him.

"Can we play again?"

"I think it's about your bedtime. I need you up early in the morning."

"Dad, can I sleep in your bedroom tonight?"

"With me? You're a bit big for that. What's all this about? You haven't slept with me for a long time. Are you sickening for something?" He touched Jamie's forehead.

"I don't feel that well."

"I'll bring you a malted drink. I think once you're in bed you'll fall asleep. Your eyes look tired. Too much time at that computer screen. Come on. Let's clear this lot away. Then you can go up and use the bathroom."

Jamie stood up from the settee. "I don't feel that well, Dad. Will you come up with me?"

"Jamie, you look quite capable to me. Go upstairs and call me when you're in bed."

Jamie edged round the door into the hall. The hall light was on but not the light to the landing upstairs. He walked slowly to the foot of the stairs, checking the kitchen door and glancing at the front door. There were too many entrances. It could come from anywhere.

He reached the top of the stairs. The bedroom doors were closed, but for his Dad's. What if he opened his own door to find.... He tried not to think about it. No, it would be safer in his Dad's bedroom. It wouldn't look for him there.

The duvet on his Dad's double bed was deep and soft. Peach and plum shapes swirled across the surface - his mum's favourite colours. Even the curtains carried the same hues. The wallpaper was... He tried to remember the colour... off white. No, like an elephant's tusk – ivory – ivory white. He remembered his mum smiling when she chose it. "Ivory like my wedding dress," she said. She'd kept that in the wardrobe cocooned in cellophane.

"Where are you? I've got the drink." Jamie's Dad appeared at the top of the stairs. "I'll put it on the bedside table in your bedroom. Have you used the bathroom?"

Jamie didn't answer. He lingered in the bedroom doorway, his hard trainers nudging the deep, pink pile of the carpet.

"You still here? Go on then, get in the bed. But if you start snoring I'll march you back to your own room."

Jamie snuggled under the deep duvet. He could hear his Dad in the kitchen below. The late night radio programme babbled. The light from the landing shone onto the dressing table, catching the tip of the photo frame, lighting up his mother's face. He felt safe

41

CHAPTER NINE

SCHOOL FRIGHT

"Jamie are you never getting up?" his Dad stood in the doorway of the bedroom. "Jamie!"

A grunting noise came from below the cover. Then a tired face appeared above the duvet.

"Come on, you'll never make it to school today. Down in ten minutes, or no breakfast."

"Dad," Jamie called as his Dad turned to go, "Can I stay at home?"

"Why?"

"I don't feel well."

His Dad reached forward with his hand to feel Jamie's forehead. "You're not hot. Come on, school."

"Dad, I feel ill."

"Jamie, I have to have a day off work with you if you stay at home. Come on, son, if you do feel really ill at school you can phone me. I mean really ill. I'm not coming out because you don't fancy maths."

"Dad."

"Jamie, get out of bed and we'll see how you are. Do you feel sick?"

"No."

"Have you got a pain?"

"No."

"Well, come on."

Jamie's Dad ran downstairs. "You'll have to have toast for breakfast."

Jamie pushed the duvet aside and sat on the edge of the bed, his feet dangling to the floor. His heel caught on something. He pulled his legs up again, squatting on the mattress. Then he hung over the edge and peered underneath the bed. Nothing. He'd survived the night but this thing from Legendworld was going to arrive sometime.

"Right, if you're really ill phone me, okay?" Jamie's Dad called from the car, as he dropped Jamie off at the school gate. "See you tonight."

Jamie waved as his Dad drove off. Then he ran quickly into the playground to join his friends. If something from Legendworld were coming he would be safe amongst a crowd.

"You're late again," said Louise. "We're just going in."

Jamie ran into the cloakroom. He tried to hang up his coat with the others. It fell to the floor. A rucksack caught his back as he stooped down. He jumped up, fighting off the bulging bag. In the shadows of the coats he thought he saw a movement. He stood motionless waiting for the tentacle to appear. The door to the classroom was only a few metres away. He ought to run but his legs wouldn't move.

Suddenly a beam of light filled the corridor. His eyes were tortured by the glare from the playground. A large shadow began to fill the open doorway. All was black. Jamie held his eyes tightly closed and stood motionless. Perhaps if he didn't see it, it wouldn't see him.

"Are you going to stand there all day blocking this corridor?" a voice boomed out.

Jamie opened his eyes. Before him was the huge figure of Mrs. Prom. "Stop this play acting, this minute! What is this all about? Now get your things and go to your classroom."

"What's the matter with you?" Louise asked, as she took a hymnbook from the pile. "You've said nothing all morning."

"Nothing?" said Jamie.

"There, you're still saying nothing." Louise laughed.

"You will need a hymn book this morning," said Miss Foster. "You don't know this hymn. Jessica lead off please." The well formed line crocodiled towards the hall doors.

Inside the hall children were seated, lips sealed, bottoms velcroed to the floor. Mrs. Bright, the Head-teacher, paraded in front of the infants nodding and smiling. Then she turned to an older girl who dared to use her voice. "Sandra, stand up, please. See me at the end of assembly. You know the rules."

Jamie wriggled in-between Louise and Sam. Their knees collided as he tried to keep his Buddha like position. Sam nudged back, fighting for extra centimetres of floor space.

"Now we are all here, I think we can welcome our guest for this morning's assembly," said Mrs. Bright. "Welcome in your usual way - Mr. Dierling."

Dierling! Jamie looked up at the tall man in the grey suit. Was this the Dierling? The school broke into loud hand clapping. Louise tried to nudge Jamie into action but he pulled his knees up tight and wedged himself between his friends then lowered his head and shoulders, hiding behind Jake. Somehow he had to hide. Dierling from Legendworld, this was all too real.

"And Mr. Dierling is here to present certificates to our lucky prize winners. You all remember the competition to write the best Football Story." The Head Teacher's voice droned in Jamie's head. "The competition is linked between Nottingham Forest and Save the Children. This morning Mr. Dierling, representing Save the Children, will give out certificates. And this afternoon he will take the children down to Nottingham Forest to have their photos taken with the team and receive, oh lots of nice things. Well over to you Mr. Dierling."

"Good morning children," said Mr. Dierling.

Jamie looked everywhere except towards the stage.

"Let's get started straight away, and the first award is to ...."

"It's you Jamie, go up." Louise pushed Jamie's arm. "Go on."

Jamie looked from side to side.

"Jamie, go out." Louise pushed him again.

Jamie knew there was no escape. If he flew for the door someone would chase him.

"Jamie," Dierling repeated the name.

"Go on," said Louise, pushing his legs.

"Come out Jamie," said the Head Teacher, waving her arm. "There's nothing to be afraid of. I'm sure Mr. Dierling's not going to carry you away," and she laughed.

Jamie walked between the rows to the end. He could see Dierling holding the certificate towards him, his tall figure dwarfing Mrs. Bright, the pale grey suit contrasting against the sunflower yellow walls.

"Well done." Dierling shook Jamie's hand.

Jamie looked at the floor, avoiding his gaze.

"A very good piece of writing. We can talk more about it this afternoon."

Jamie felt his fingers slide from the firm grip. He plucked the certificate from Dierling's hand and walked to the other side behind Mrs. Bright.

"Anthea." The role-call continued, as one by one the other five children came forward to collect their prizes. Jamie stared straight ahead watching the ducks, painted cream and white, floating on the frieze at the back of the hall. He clutched his certificate in perspiring palms.

"Now, this afternoon………"

Jamie began to feel strange. The voices around him became blurred. The ducks began to fade.

"Are you all right, Jamie?" a voice called from above him. "Jamie!"

"I think he's coming to," another voice added. "Jamie."

Jamie opened his eyes. Mrs. Bright and Miss Foster were staring down at him. His hand touched the polished floor.

"Good job someone caught you," said Mrs. Bright. "You could have had a nasty bump on your head. We'll try to sit you up, come on." Mrs. Bright took one arm and Miss Foster took the other.

"There, how's that?" They helped him to a chair at the side of the hall. Jamie could see the rows of faces. Some children were applauding. Dierling was still there.

"I'll get the secretary to ring your Dad," said Mrs. Bright. "Maybe you ought to go home. You look very pale." She felt Jamie's forehead. "A little perspiration, better get you comfortable in your own bed."

"Well, when you do it, you do it in style. You managed to get me home," said Jamie's Dad, as he pushed open the front door of their house. "Come on in. We'd better get you sorted out. A nice warm bed is what they suggested."

"I'm all right now," said Jamie. "I can sit in a chair."

"And watch T.V." His Dad laughed. "No you don't – bed. I haven't come home from work for you to sit watching T.V all afternoon. Bed. Then if you're no better I'll phone your Grandad and he'll take you to the doctor tomorrow."

"Here you are, boiled egg with bread and butter fingers. Are you feeling better? You've had a good sleep this afternoon. But don't get too attached to my bed. I think you'll be sleeping in your own bed tonight." Jamie's Dad set the tray down on the coffee table in the lounge.

"Dad, do you think people can come from websites?"

"If they work for a company that has a website. Yes. Now, eat up everything. I've put some raisins in a tub. They're full of iron."

Jamie picked a raisin from the tub. "Dad, has anyone ever emailed a person across the Internet?"

"Not that I know of. That would be the day. I can think of a few people I'd like to email into outer space."

"But, do you think you could? And can you stop people coming...?"

"Jamie, forget about computers for a while. Eat your food and build up your strength."

"Dad, can we watch the news?"

"I think you'll be waiting a few hours. It was on earlier when you were still in bed."

"Has Danny come back?"

"Sorry, don't know. I didn't watch it."

"Is there anything in the newspaper about Danny?"

"I didn't buy one. Didn't have time. Now stop worrying about him. All the worrying in the world won't bring him back."

"You're not bothered about him!"

"Jamie, I'm sure he's a very nice young man and...."

"You don't care because you don't like football."

"There's the telephone." Jamie's Dad stood up from the settee and went into the hall to answer it.

"Hello there, how are things in the Youth Team? Jamie, it's your cousin Kevin on the phone for you. Hang on Kev, we've an invalid in our midst. He could be some time getting to the phone."

"I'm all right." Jamie stood up. "Tell him I'm coming."

"Looks like a miraculous recovery." Jamie's Dad laughed and handed the phone to him.

"Where were you this afternoon?" asked Kevin. "I thought you were coming to the ground to get some award."

"I fainted in school and Dad had to take me home. Dad says I've got to go to the doctors for a check up tomorrow morning. Then I have to go back to school in the afternoon."

"Hope you'll be well for Thursday night's match. Remember it's an important game."

"Is Danny back?" asked Jamie.

"Not that I know of."

"It won't be worth going on Thursday if Danny's not playing," said Jamie.

"That's not fighting talk. You can come and watch me play."

"Are you playing for the First Team?"

"Looks like it."

"Are you substitute for Danny?"

"No, they've got an injured player as well."

"We can't win without Danny," said Jamie.

"Think positive. We will win. We're going out there to win and I'd better hear you cheering the loudest!"

Friar Tuck patted his huge stomach and sighed contentedly. It had been a delicious day of banqueting in Nottingham. Now he would curl up in his blanket and sleep for the night. There really wasn't any need to chase after Danny. He knew where he was - at Nottingham Forest Football Club. And he would still be there tomorrow.

"Why waste good eating time?" the Friar thought to himself. "There's so much lovely food to be eaten in this new city. Danny isn't going anywhere and I don't need to get him back to the Medieval Forest until Friday. I think I'll just linger for a while. I think I could just manage another one of those delicious hot, burning lamb dinners. I'm sure Legendworld won't miss this money from their bag."

He pulled out a purse and counted the coins. "Yes, and maybe a nice tray of those fried potatoes for supper. I'll go to the football ground tomorrow when I've had a sizzling bacon breakfast and maybe a small midday meal of one of those splendid hot beef patties."

CHAPTER TEN

STICKY BUSINESS

"Special Wednesday afternoon delivery – one recovered boy. Sorry he was away this morning but we thought we'd better have him checked out at the doctor's." Jamie's Grandad stood in the cloakroom doorway, his hand round Jamie's shoulder.

"This is great," Miss Foster beamed. "You're just back in time. I've had Mr. Dierling on the phone and he says if Jamie's back he'll collect him this afternoon. You're to have your own private tour of Nottingham Forest Football Club, Jamie."

"That'll suit you," said Jamie's Grandad. "Good job you came back this afternoon."

Jamie gripped his school bag tightly. "I don't feel too well, Grandad."

"You'll be fine. The doctor said you were fine. I'll see you tomorrow at the match. Bye Miss Foster."

Jamie waved to his Grandad. He knew there was no way out of this.

"I'll just go and phone Mr. Dierling." Miss Foster headed off down the corridor. "Wait there, Jamie. I bet he'll be round straight away."

"So we meet again." Dierling held out his hand. Jamie kept his hand at his side. "Well, no time for exaggerated manners, lets away. I'll bring him back before the end of school, Miss Foster."

"Fine. You couldn't just take another twenty five?" She waved her hand towards the rest of the class.

"Sorry, maybe another day. Come on Jamie," and Dierling guided Jamie towards the door. Out in the corridor Jamie walked on ahead. "This way," Dierling called, opening the door out into the car park. "We'd better move quickly. There's a photographer waiting."

Jamie froze. Photographer, was Dierling going to email him to Legendworld?

"Jamie are you going?" Mrs Foster saw him hesitating in the corridor.

"I don't feel very well." Jamie tried to stagger.

"Oh dear!" Miss Foster ran forward.

"I'm sure he'll manage half an hour," said Dierling, scooping him up and carrying him to the door.

"Are you sure?" Miss Foster called out.

"Quite sure. We'll push him in the wheelchair if he shows signs of staggering again."

"Okay, now?" Dierling settled Jamie into the seat of the green people - carrier then climbed into his own seat. He pushed the gear lever into reverse and started to back across the playground. "Perhaps the doctor will do some tests on you to sort out these fainting fits. Please use your seat belt."

Jamie pulled the harness over and secured the catch then sat waiting. "Are you comfortable?" Dierling asked, as the vehicle swung out of the school gate into the road.

"Yes, thank you," said Jamie.

"Very good, we're on our way."

Jamie's mind began to race. Emails, photographs – zooming through space and time or even... He held on to the seat, waiting for the car to launch into the sky and soar above Nottingham like a huge green dragon, headlights for eyes. Instead the car suddenly stopped forcefully. Jamie felt himself being flung forward. The safety harness locked.

"Sorry about that," said Dierling. "These people will not signal at roundabouts. Are you alright?"

"Yes."

"Good job you're strapped in. Can never be too safe. It pays to think before you do anything. Prepare yourself for the unknown. Take all precautions when you are about to make a journey, or prepare a journey for someone else."

Jamie shuffled in his seat. His gaze turned to the window.

Dierling continued, "I've known so many journeys fail or become a catastrophe when people have not taken precautions. Are you a cautious person, Jamie?" Jamie turned from the window not knowing how to answer.

"Do you think long and hard before you embark on a new project?"

Jamie said nothing.

"I think it's good to show initiative," said Dierling. "But sometimes you need to research a little before you actually push the button. Here we are." He swung into the gateway of Nottingham Forest ground. "We've made it, safe and sound."

Jamie released the seat belt. Dierling turned to him. "I can't say I'm pleased with your emailing adventures, Jamie, but what is done is done. We must now deal with the consequences. Your attempts to return Danny Lacey to this world have failed. Even more serious, you have managed to activate a Legendworld creature and invite it into your world. And I believe we will find it inside this building."

A Legendworld creature.... Jamie wasn't sure he could handle any more visitors from Legendworld.

"Mr. Dierling!" Someone banged on the car door. "The photographer's here now."

"We'll be out," Dierling signalled. "Come on, Jamie, time to go."

"Hello young man. How are you feeling?" Mr. Furse, the club's Marketing Manager, met them at the door.

"I think he's recovered now," said Dierling."You're okay aren't you Jamie?"

"Does this sickness cause you to lose your voice?" Mr. Furse laughed. "Come on, anyway.

We're going to the trophy room to have your photo taken. Not quite all the team. But we've got four players."

Jamie had no chance to turn back as Dierling took his arm and followed Mr. Furse to the door of the Trophy room.

"They're all waiting for you," said Mr. Furse, as he pushed open the door. Four footballers, in kit, were standing at a glass cabinet filled with trophies. A man in a suit stepped forward. Mr. Furse introduced him as the Team Manager.

"Hello young man. Better not shake your hand or we'll stick together. I don't know what's stuck on that cabinet door but I can't get it off my fingers. It's all over the lock. I'll have to get someone to give it a clean."

Mr. Furse looked at the cabinet. "It's like a mesh, a spiders web. Has someone been using glue from a very fine nozzle?"

"Don't know," said the Manager. "But we can't have the lock damaged. There are too many prize possessions in that cabinet. See that football." He took Jamie to the glass. "Very special. All the signatures of the Nottingham Forest and Manchester United players are on that ball. Last game Manchester United team played before they were killed in an air crash in Germany – very special." He rubbed his fingers together again. "You get on with the photo. I'll go and see what I can do about this glue."

"Come on then." Mr. Furse took Jamie to join the players. "Lots of smiles for the camera."

Dierling fingered the doorframe of the glass cabinet. Jamie could see him pulling out glue threads and putting them onto a piece of paper.

"That's it, let's have you in close," the photographer called out to the players. "Just a bit closer – smile." The camera flashed. Dierling left the room carrying his find.

"Right, we'd better get on with the tour of the club," said Mr. Furse. "Thanks for your time." He waved to the players as they left. Jamie watched the door swing closed behind them.

"Could I just have a word with Jamie before you start?" Dierling was back in the room. "It won't take a moment." Dierling took Jamie to one side. "Now, I must ask you one question Jamie. What were the exact words of your last email message to Legendworld?"

"I don't know. I can't remember exactly... Mr. Dierling, what's in the club? Where's the creature from Legendworld?"

"That's what I'm trying to find out," said Dierling, "and I need your help, Jamie. Now please think. What did you say in your email?"

"I think I said 'Please send Danny Lacey back to Nottingham Forest Football Club'."

"Lacey, are you sure you spelt it correctly?"

"I don't know."

"It only takes one letter to be changed."

"I don't know. I thought I typed Lacey."

"Lacey, Laceb, Laced, Lacef." Dierling began to go through the alphabet.

"Are you ready, now?" asked Mr. Furse. "I think we should get started."

"Quite," said Dierling.

Mr. Furse pushed open the door. "I'm sure you'll want to look at the players' changing room, Jamie. It's this way."

Dierling followed on, still devising names. "Lacep. Lacer. Lacer!" he shouted out aloud.

Mr. Furse gave him a puzzled smile and banged on a door. "You must always check changing rooms in case anyone's in. It's all right we can go in."

Jamie ventured in past the rows of trainers stacked on the shelf inside the door. Something nudged his shoulder. He jumped round to face Dierling. The trainers began to topple to the floor.

"Whoops, better catch these." Dierling reached out to stop the avalanche.

Mr. Furse joined in the rescue. "Ugh! What's this sticky mess?" He tried to free his fingers from the interlaced shoes, throwing them back on the stack.

"Jamie," Dierling whispered from behind, "its as I thought." He pointed to the meshed trainers. "The Lacer is here."

"What's a Lacer? Where is it?"

"Judging by this trail it is not far away." Dierling tried to rub the sticky secretion from his fingers.

"Perhaps we should go out on the pitch," said Mr. Furse, wiping his fingers on a tissue and walking back into the passageway.

"We must follow the trail," Dierling whispered to Jamie. "We need to find the Lacer creature, itself, before the Disposer is activated."

"What do you mean?" asked Jamie. "What's a Disposer? How many Legendworld creatures are there in the Club?"

"Hello, is this another visitor?" a lady, pushing a large plastic trolley, appeared in the hallway.

"It's a celebratory tour," said Mr. Furse. "Jamie, this is Jan."

"Do you want to see the centre of this universe?" asked Jan. "Follow me and I'll take you to my little world."

"I'm not sure we've got time," said Mr. Furse."

"I'm sure Jamie would love to see all the team shirts," said Dierling, feeling the sticky edge of the trolley.

"I'm not sure," said Jamie. "I feel a bit…"

"Come on," said Dierling. "You've got the chance to see the players' full kit."

"Well, everybody to the laundry then." Mr. Furse led the way down the corridor.

"I warn you, it's very hot," said Jan, as they came to the door. "You'll think you're on an African Safari."

"I don't mind a little heat," said Dierling. "How about you Jamie. Can you survive five minutes in the Drying Room?"

When Jan opened the door the warm air hit them and the loud noise of the washing machine's whir filled their ears.

"Step in," said Jan. "The Drying Room with all the shirts is on the left."

Dierling was the first to put his head round the door. "Now this is worth a visit." He beckoned Jamie to follow him.

"It's all right," said Jamie. "I'll wait here." He stood close to Mr. Furse.

The Drying Room had no windows. Rows of tracksuits hung on steel coat hangers, on moveable trolleys. Dierling pushed a trolley full of clothes to one side. "It's very warm in here."

"Like the Bahamas!" Jan called out, laughing.

"I don't think I'd chose to stay a week in there," said Mr. Furse.

"I think not," said Dierling, fingering the Lacer's glue on one of the tracksuit tops. "I don't think anyone would want to spend a night in here."

"Won't get a chance," said Jan. "It's locked up. If you get in there, you'll have to stay 'til the morning. You'll have to bring your own sandwiches."

"I don't think we'll be staying for supper," said Mr. Furse. "How about looking at the pitch now, Jamie?"

Dierling lingered in the doorway. "You go on. I just want to talk to Jan."

"It's just the two of us, then." Mr. Furse led Jamie down the corridor. "Here we are." He opened the door with a key. "Come on Jamie."

All thoughts of Legendworld disappeared as Jamie walked through the players tunnel. He could see the huge Brian Clough stand in front, the red seats rising to the sky. He wanted to run - run on to the pitch and score a goal.

"We'll have a little walk round the edge," said Mr. Furse. "We've got excellent turf this season. I think it's as green as Ireland, the Emerald Isle."

"Some sight isn't it!" Dierling came down from the tunnel to join them. "All that red and green."

"Yes, I was just saying we've got a great pitch this year," said Mr. Furse. "And a great team."

"Very commendable," said Dierling. "Now, Jamie, I think it's time we were getting back. Thank you, Mr. Furse, for the private tour. I'm sure you'll want to thank Mr. Furse, Jamie."

"Thank you." Jamie looked up from his gaze at the stadium.

"Thank you again for all your support." Dierling shook Mr. Furse's hand. "The Charity appreciates all that you've done."

"No trouble and remember to book your free match ticket, Jamie." said Mr. Furse. "Bye."

In the car park Dierling opened the vehicle door. Jamie jumped into the seat and closed the door firmly behind him. Dierling climbed in the drivers seat and started the engine.

"That was a good afternoon. Nice people." Dierling reversed, then swung the car towards the exit. "Remember to order your free ticket."

Jamie was confused. Why hadn't Dierling said anymore about Danny? He needed to know if Danny was safe.

"Where's Danny?" Jamie blurted the words out.

"Danny's quite safe in Legendworld. I simply have to locate him." Dierling watched the traffic as he turned out into the road.

"You've got to find him now," said Jamie.

"I don't think Danny is our priority at this moment," said Dierling.

"But he's got to be back by Thursday or we'll lose the match!"

"If we don't find the Lacer there could be no match," said Dierling.

"What will the Lacer do?"

"Nothing. It's all done," said Dierling.

"What do you mean?"

"The Lacer laces together anything in its path in preparation for the Disposer."

"What's a Disposer? What does a Disposer do?"

"Well, in simple terms, he eats his supper. Trainers, tracksuits, trophies - everything the Lacer has worked on."

"People?" asked Jamie.

"If they sit still long enough," said Dierling.

"Would he eat the players?"

"People, football players, anyone and anything. That's why I will have to activate the Trawl as soon as possible before the Disposer comes out looking for his supper."

"What's the Trawl?" asked Jamie.

"It's a very convenient Legendworld retrieval system," said Dierling. "When something has been missing from Legendworld for some time the Trawl is activated. It often appears as a bright light. It captures the creature and transports it back to Legendworld. But anything close by is captured too."

"Can the Trawl catch people if they are near the creature?" asked Jamie.

"I'm afraid so. It can be very upsetting to be accidentally transported to Legendworld."

"But if you use the Trawl to catch the Lacer and it's in the changing rooms, you could catch some of the players as well," said Jamie.

"Yes, there is that risk," said Dierling, as they drove down the road towards the school.

"But you can't take that risk," said Jamie. "We can't lose any more players. We haven't got Danny back yet. Can't you just take a photo of the Lacer and Disposer and email them to Legendworld?"

"That's what I intended to do this afternoon," said Dierling. "But the Lacer is far too small and the Disposer will not come out until nearer dark - probably this evening. That gives me time to get things organised."

"Don't take the whole team to Legendworld," Jamie pleaded.

"Don't worry. Leave it to me, Jamie. I shall manage things very carefully. The Lacer and Disposer will be back in Legendworld before breakfast. Here we are." Dierling turned into the school playground. "Safe and sound. I hope you enjoyed your visit. And if I were you I'd stay away from your computer for a few days. Let me sort out all the Legendworld business."

Dierling waved as he pulled away from the school car park. Jamie stood thinking. The Trawl, Dierling was going to activate the Trawl. There wasn't much time. He would have to take things into his own hands again. They couldn't risk losing any more players before Thursday.

CHAPTER ELEVEN

THE DISPOSER

Jamie checked for his camera in his pocket then pulled his bike from the wall. He would have to move fast before his Dad saw him.

"Hey, where are you shooting off to?" Too late, his Dad was at the front door already. "I don't want you going too far. I want you home in a reasonable time ready for bed."

"I'm.." Jamie hesitated. He knew his Dad wouldn't let him cycle across town to the football ground. "I'm going to call in on Grandad." That wasn't a lie because he could call to see his Grandad on the way back.

"Well, just you be careful on the roads. And whilst you're there tell him I've bought that piece of fencing."

"Ah," the Friar yawned and stretched. A passer by in the street almost fell over his legs. He patted his huge stomach and sat upright on the pavement. Another shopper threw some pennies at his feet and smiled.

The Friar wiped the last crumbs from his mouth and felt into his pocket for the jam doughnuts. "Yes, two left," he thought to himself. "I will keep those for later. The search for Robin might be long and hazardous. I will need sustenance."

"Can you please move your feet?" A young woman with a pushchair stood beside him.

"Oh, I am indeed sorry." The Friar pulled himself up from the floor.

"Thank you," said the woman. " Perhaps you should go back to the 'Tales of Robin Hood', now." The Friar nodded politely. Had she recognised him already? He would have to move fast. No more eating. It was time to find Danny. He would ask the way from the shops to Nottingham Forest Football Club.

Jamie propped his bike against the wall near the football club. He wouldn't need to stay long, just long enough to get into the club and take the photos. Maybe no one would see him if he went round the back.

"Hey, Jamie, what are you doing here?" his cousin, Kevin, ran towards him from the football pitch.

"I've... I've left a book inside. I've come to pick it up. I left it this afternoon when I came to look round."

"So you got your own private tour. Did you have a good time?"

"Yes... Kev, can I come in with you?"

"I suppose so. You won't be long will you?"

"No. I just need to look in a couple of rooms."

"As long as you stay near the changing rooms. Or did you leave it in the trophy room? You won't get in there without permission."

"No, I think I dropped it before we went out to see the pitch." Jamie's lie grew.

"Come on, then," said Kevin. "Watch out or you'll get trampled by this herd of elephants!" Three young players ran past Jamie.

"Did you have your photo taken?" Kevin led Jamie towards the tunnel.

"Yes."

"You'll have to get me a copy. Well, let's get in. I've got to get changed. Are you sure you didn't leave your book in the trophy room? You can't get back in there tonight."

"No, it's somewhere along this corridor."

"How about this trolley?" Kevin rolled the pink plastic trolley. "Not much in there. Don't go astray. I'm in that room if you want me. Did you want to look in the changing room?" Kevin pushed the door open. There was a barrage of voices. Someone had set the showers running and there was the sound of singing in the hollow washroom.

"I think I'll look along the corridor," said Jamie.

"Okay, don't get into any trouble. I'll meet you outside in five minutes." Kevin disappeared into the changing room.

Jamie pulled a piece of paper from his pocket, the photo of the Lacer downloaded from the website. Dierling was right it was miniscule. This wouldn't be easy.

"Hello, young man! You look a bit young to be training with this squad."

Jamie turned at the sound of Jan's voice. "I'm looking for something," he stuttered.

"Looking for something? And does anyone know you're here?" asked Jan.

"My cousin Kevin brought me in. He's getting changed."

"Oh Kevin, the comedian, so you're his cousin. And are you a Nottingham Forest supporter?"

"Yes."

"So, you'll have your tickets for the big match on Thursday?"

"Yes."

"What is it then?"

"What?"

"What you're looking for."

"It's a…. book, a book," Jamie blurted out.

"I haven't seen a book in here. How would your book get in here?"

"I came to look round this afternoon."

"Oh, yes, now I remember you. You were with that man from the charity organisation. You had a private tour. Well, I don't think I've seen anything. But you can have a quick look. You can peep in this room where I hang the tracksuits – but don't stay long, it's like a sauna."

Jamie peered into the Drying Room. "Dierling was very interested in this room," he thought to himself, as he looked at the rows of tracksuits hanging on the rails. "Are they sticky?" He reached out to touch one. "Uhg!" He pulled back. The tracksuit top was sticky. The whole row of tops was laced together by the fine sticky thread. The secretion was still wet. He knew the lacer was here somewhere. He needed time to search without being disturbed. Jan was wiping down the huge automatic washer. He wanted her to go into the other room.

"No luck then?" Jan peered into the Drying Room.

"No," said Jamie, freeing his fingers from the glue.

"Well, if I see it I'll pass it on to your cousin."

"Thank you," said Jamie, going out into the corridor. He knew he would have to wait until Jan left the laundry before he could get back into the Drying Room again.

"Don't hang around too long on your own," said Jan. "They'll be locking up soon, once everyone's out of the shower. Then you'll have to go round the other way."

Jamie walked slowly to the exit door, as slowly as he could.

The Friar's sandals slapped against the tarmac car park. He was at the club at last. He rested against the wall near the Reception Entrance. The walk to the stadium had been longer than he expected. But he'd made it.

"Have you lost your way?" a young man called as he got out of his car. "Is this a stunt for tonight? I think you'll be wanting the Robin Hood Suite with that costume!" He laughed and walked off.

Robin Hood Suite! The friar reacted quickly. He tightened his rope belt and shuffled after the young man.

"Are you going to entertain everyone?" the young man asked, turning to the Friar.

"Well..." but before the Friar could frame an answer the young man spoke again.

"Here we are." He pointed to the glass doors of a new building. The Friar looked up. Above the door of the building was a name 'The Robin Hood Suite'.

"Go in," said the young man. "I'm sure they'll make you welcome. I'm not coming back until things start." He pushed open the door and beckoned for the Friar to enter. "Hey, and don't eat all those trifles before I get back!"

The room was set out like a banquet. There were long tables topped with a rich array of foods: filled rolls, chicken legs and five wonderful fruit and cream trifles. "Well," thought the Friar. "I'm here now and I've got plenty of time to find Robin. One small trifle will not be missed."

Jamie loitered in the corridor near the Laundry Room. He kept a close eye on Jan. As soon as she walked off in the other direction he crept back towards the Drying Room. The washing machine still whirred. Now was his chance. He darted through the door, almost pulling down a row of tracksuits. The light was on so he could see to begin his search for the Lacer.

"See you!" a voice called out in the corridor.
"Hey, Jan, have you seen my cousin?" Jamie recognised Kevin's voice.
"Yes, but he's gone now," Jan called back.
"I should think he's gone home," said Kevin. "Thanks Jan, watch the washing!"

Jamie heard Kevin's footsteps down the corridor. Jan laughed after him. Her laughter grew louder as she walked into the Laundry Room. No. Jamie knew he had to hide quickly. He hid behind the rail of tracksuits, trying to tuck himself between the tops. Jan's face appeared in the doorway of the Drying Room. Then the room went dark as she switched off the light. Darkness became total darkness as the door closed and Jamie heard the key turn in the lock.

The Friar set down the empty trifle dish and wiped his mouth with his sleeve. "I will have to be careful. People are recognising me and they may warn Robin that I am on my way," he thought out aloud.

He looked round the room. So much delicious food, but he had to find a disguise. There was no more time for banqueting. He staggered towards the outer door of the Robin Hood Suite, custard and jelly smeared across his fat stomach and gateau crumbs caked to his chin. He pushed the two chicken legs deeper into his pocket.

Outside the room he saw a young woman heading towards him. He darted quickly through a door that led to an office. "No use staying here," he thought. "I must find Robin. But first I must find a disguise."

Jamie pushed on the Drying Room door. It was locked securely. There was no way out. Something was snuffling in the darkness. The sound was coming from the floor near his feet. It grew louder. Now it was behind him. He felt a pull on his tee shirt and jumped round, knocking over clothes stands in his panic. His scalp tingled as if his hair was standing on end. Something was pulling, sucking him upwards.

He grabbed out at the clothes as his feet left the floor. His fingers groped for a hold to anchor him down. The coat hangers twisted, tracksuits crumpled.

The whole stand was pulled from the floor. Everything he touched was rising with him, sucked higher and higher towards the dark corner of the ceiling.

Well it would have to do. Friar Tuck adjusted Sherwood Bear's head. It was hot inside the bear's costume. The head slipped on easily but he found it very warm and he couldn't see properly. But it would have to do. He was thankful that he'd come across that room and found the suit hanging on a hook. Nobody would recognise him now. He could search for Robin without anyone disturbing him.

"Hey you don't need to practise wearing that outfit!" a lean youth shouted, as he ran past the Friar in the passageway. "I didn't know you loved that mascot's outfit so much. Are you taking it home to sleep in?" The youth banged on the bear's head and ran towards the exit door.

"Ugh," the Friar groaned as he pulled the bear's head off. "Ah," a final sigh of relief as he dropped the head to the floor. It grinned up at him. Now he should concentrate on finding Robin. "Robin!" he shouted. "Where are you? Come out of hiding. I've come to help you!"

Jamie heard the Friar's voice. "Help! Help me!" he shouted back, as he clung to the clothes stand

.

wedged in the corner of the ceiling of the Drying Room.

"Robin is that you?" The Friar tugged on the handle of the Laundry Room door. "Don't worry, I'll save you! I'll get this door open – just you see!"

"Help! Help!" Jamie screamed out again.

"Hold on. I'll have to use this Legendworld bracelet. Let me see. This one?" he pressed one of the gold keys on the bracelet around his wrist. "Come on, do something." He tried another key. "Stupid contraption!" he shouted in frustration.

"Help, Help!" Jamie screamed from behind the wall.

"I'm coming! I'm coming! Just let me read these instructions." The Friar stared hard at the screen that popped up from the bracelet. "To go through walls," he read out aloud. "Aim the wristlet at the proposed wall and press the red key." The friar pressed the key. "Ah!" he yelled as his feet rose from the ground and he found himself hurtling towards the wall. "No!" For one brief second the wall disappeared. The Friar bounced against pipes, wrestled with steaming washing and finally landed with a thud on the floor of the Drying Room.

"I'm up here!" Jamie shouted out from above him. "Help me!"

The Friar looked up blindly into the darkness. "Robin!" he shouted. "I can't see you. Where?... Ah!" The friar grabbed out for the clothes rail as once again he felt himself rising from the floor. His fingers stuck to the Lacers glue. The whole rail of washing lifted up with him. Friar and washing drifted to the ceiling. "No, no!" the Friar shrieked in horror. "It's the Disposer!"

"Hey!" Jamie shouted, as the full weight of the Friars bulk slammed into him.

"So sorry. I'm afraid things are out of my control. Just a minute." The Friar puffed and panted as he kicked out and anchored his feet against the wall, wedging himself in the corner.

"I can't hold on much longer!" said Jamie. "If I let go of this rail I'll be sucked up. What is this thing?"

"You are at the mouth of the biggest vacuum cleaner in the Universe. If you let go you'll be sucked into a bag and... I don't like to think about it. Quick, grab my leg!"

"I can't see your leg!"

"Well, grab any part of my body. Just hang on tight. I'm going to get us out of here right now."

Jamie reached out into the darkness.

"Ow!" the Friar winced. "I didn't say pinch a handful of my flesh. Just hold onto my sleeve. Have you got a good grip?"

"It's hard. I can't hold on to you and the clothes rail."

"Just two seconds. This is guesswork in the dark. Yes, it's illuminated! Right, press the red key.

Hang on, Robin, we are about to fly through the wall."
……

"Oh! Always hard landings!" The Friar bounced onto the floor in the corridor. He sat up and looked at Jamie. "Are you okay? You're not Robin!"

"I didn't say I was called Robin." Jamie tried to pull himself up but the tracksuit was still stuck to his fingers.

"Erh, the Lacer is such a messy creature." The Friar tugged a shirt from his tunic.

"We've come through the wall," said Jamie, throwing the tracksuit on the ground and at last freeing himself. "How did you do that?"

"This little device." The Friar held up his wrist.

"A bracelet?"

"That bracelet saved you from the Disposer's jaws. I tell you that's the closest I've been to the Disposer. We were very lucky to escape and I'm not waiting around for it to start vacuuming up this corridor. Come on. This is not a safe place. Let's go." The Friar stood up and began to walk down the corridor.

"But it's still there," said Jamie.

"That's why I'm not staying."

"But what will happen when people come in the morning."

"He will be on snooze," said the Friar. "Come on. Nighttime is Disposer time. Tomorrow's another day. I've no doubt the Trawl will be activated in the morning. I must remember to take this with me." He picked up Sherwood Bear's head from the floor. "Now, get ready, we're going through another wall. Hold on to me. Let's hope we have a more pleasant landing."

"I wish you'd use doors," said Jamie, as they tumbled onto the green turf of the football pitch.

"Oh!" the Friar groaned. "This space travel is too much for me." He began to undo his bear suit. "And this outfit's not exactly made for speed. Make a good Antarctic suit. I shall be glad when I have found Robin and we are safely back in the forest."

"What are you talking about?" asked Jamie.

"Maybe you know where he is," said the Friar. "Time is beginning to run out." He pulled himself up from the grass. "I assure you my intentions are honourable. It is for his own good."

"I don't know anyone called Robin. Why are you wearing Sherwood Bear's suit?"

"Sherwood. So the suit does have an owner. Don't worry I shall return it tomorrow evening. Are you sure you don't remember seeing Robin? He.." the Friar had a sudden thought. "No, not Robin. He now goes by the name of Danny. Yes, Danny."

"Danny!" Jamie stood upright. "Do you mean Danny Lacer?"

"I only know he calls himself Danny - Danny the football player. Wait, I have a picture of him." The Friar pulled a Nottingham Forest Match Programme

.

from inside the bear suit. "There he is." He pointed to a full team photo.

"It is Danny Lacey you're talking about," said Jamie. " Why do you want Danny?"

"I am one of Robin's...I mean Danny's dearest friends and I have come to deliver him back to the Forest."

"You're not talking sense," said Jamie."

"But do you know where he is? I do not mean him any harm."

"He's.." Jamie hesitated. Could he trust this stranger? "He's missing."

"I know he's missing," said the Friar. "That's why I'm looking for him. Oh drat this disguise! It is so cumbersome." He plodded towards the gateway. "But it will keep me warm tonight. And..." he pulled a chicken leg from inside his tunic. "I have some sustenance. Goodbye my friend. You take care. I hope we'll meet again in more pleasant circumstances." He ambled off across the pitch.

Jamie pulled his bike from the wall. Who was the new mascot? Where did he get the bracelet? Why did he want Danny? Was Danny in more danger? So many questions raced through Jamie's mind. And the Disposer was still in the club. What if it was there tomorrow? But the man in the bear suit had said it wouldn't be there because someone would activate the Trawl. He knew about the Trawl. The Trawl! No the whole team could disappear. He needed to contact Dierling.

Jamie avoided his Dad's questions when he got home. He put his bike in the shed and rushed upstairs to the computer and began to type out an email message for Dierling. Maybe he should trust Dierling. He'd said he would get Danny back. Surely he wouldn't scoop up the whole team before the match. But the man in Sherwood Bear's suit? He could be dangerous. He began to write the email.

Dierling, I met a man at the Club dressed as a bear who can move through walls...

No, that didn't sound right. Anyway he couldn't tell Dierling he'd been to the Club to photograph the Lacer. Dierling had told him not to do anymore emailing.

Dierling I have met a man who says he is looking for Danny...

Jamie thought for a moment and continued writing.

But he thinks his name is Robin. This man knows about the Trawl and he carries a bracelet, which has special powers. I think Danny could be in danger.

"Come on, let's get you to bed," Jamie's Dad called from downstairs. "You've got a late night tomorrow with the football match. You'll want to feel wide-awake when your Grandad comes to collect you. Did you tell him about the fencing?"

"I forgot," said Jamie. "I'll tell him tomorrow."

Later that night Jamie tossed in a restless sleep.

His dreams were filled with giant Disposers sucking up the houses - towns - the Universe. Three Friar Tucks floated out into space, joined together by a sticky mesh, laughing and screeching as they chomped on huge turkey legs. A large silver spaceship landed in the middle of Nottingham Forest Football Stadium and out spilled the whole of the First Team.

CHAPTER TWELVE

MORE TROUBLE

"Come on sleepy head! It's not the weekend yet." Jamie's Dad woke him from his slumbers. "Down in ten minutes."

Jamie opened his tired eyes and looked at the clock. He was late. He pushed back the heavy duvet and dragged his clothes from the chair then began to get dressed. He wouldn't have time to use the bathroom. He needed to check his emails.

Jamie switched the light on in the spare room and sat, blurry eyed, in front of the computer. Would there be a message from Dierling?

"Jamie!" his Dad called from the bottom of the stairs. "I think you should come and see this on the television."

"Just a minute."

"It's serious business. The rest of the Nottingham Forest First team have gone missing now!"

"What? He's done it. Dierling's activated the Trawl!" Jamie raced down the stairs. "Dad, when did it happen? Did it happen last night?"

"Listen, the presenter's explaining everything."

"Stranger than fiction. Not one, but all of Nottingham Forest's First Team are now missing.
.

We have the Manager on the line this moment. When were the players last seen"?

"They were all present for a short time at the function in the Robin Hood Suite last night"

"When did anyone realise they were missing?"

"I had a phone call from a player's wife late last night to say that he hadn't arrived home, and she was very worried. Then we all became very worried when one by one I phoned each player and found that none of them had arrived home."

"And this morning?"

"Nothing. Not a First Team player in sight."

"Are you now convinced this is sabotage?"

"I don't like to think so. But, as you know, this is a crucial match."

"So what happens now?"

"We've been in touch with the Football Association to see if, under the circumstances, we could postpone the match. But the news is not

good. We have been advised to play our Reserve Team.”

"Reserve Team!" Jamie shouted. "We can't do that!"

"They'll have to play," said Jamie's Dad.

"That's not fair. We won't stand a chance of winning!"

"There are probably some good players in that team. That's why they're reserve."

"Dad, you don't understand!"

"Jamie, settle down now and get ready for school. You'll have to let Nottingham Forest sort out their own problems. I need to get to work. Eat this toast and let's get going."

"Who's not going to win tonight?" Tim teased, as Jamie walked into the playground. "One man gone and now you haven't got a team!"

"Don't," said Louise. "Leave him alone. Are you okay Jamie?"

"The whole team." Jamie dropped his bag on the floor. "Why did he take the whole team?"

"Who?" asked Louise.

"It's too complicated to explain," said Jamie. "I don't even understand it myself."

Jamie stared out of the classroom window. Not one player left - the whole team in Legendworld and no word from Dierling. The match was lost before it began.

"Jamie," Miss Foster interrupted his thoughts.

"Yes." He turned in his seat.

"I've some one here to see you. Says he wants a personal word."

Jamie stood up from his chair. Was it his granddad with his P.E. Kit? No, that was hanging on the peg.

"Hello, Jamie." Dierling was standing at the door. "Nice to meet you again. Is it all right if I speak to him in the corridor?" He looked at Miss Foster. She smiled and nodded. Jamie wasn't given a chance to make a choice.

"Jamie, what have you done?" asked Dierling. "I'm still trying to locate Danny and now the whole team's missing. I told you not to do any more emailing."

"I didn't. It wasn't my fault. You activated the Trawl!"

"The Trawl only netted the Lacer and the Disposer. There were no footballers."

"I didn't email anyone," said Jamie.

"Then who did?" asked Dierling.

"I bet it was the bear! It's Sherwood! I told you about him in my email. He had a photo of the whole team. He must have emailed it to Legendworld."

"Jamie, Sherwood's the mascot," said Dierling. "Why would the mascot become involved in Legendworld emailing?"

"He's not the real mascot. It's a man in disguise and he's got a special bracelet that can zoom you through walls. He knows about the Trawl. And he's looking for Danny, but he calls Danny Robin. I told you about him in my email last night."

"Slow down a minute, Jamie. I well remember your email but it left me confused. Now tell me, when did you meet this man?"

Jamie hesitated. He'd said too much. Now he had to tell Dierling about his visit to the football ground the night before.

"You had a very narrow escape last night, Jamie. I've warned you about interfering in Legendworld activities. You must leave things up to me," said Dierling

"I wanted to email a photo of the Lacer and the Disposer back to Legendworld so that you wouldn't activate the Trawl," said Jamie.

"What's done is done," said Dierling. "We must work from the present. Now, if I have it right. This man is disguised as the mascot and he carries a special bracelet which, I believe, has Legendworld powers. He doesn't sound like one of our agents so he must have stolen this equipment. You say he is searching

.

for Danny, but calls him Robin. Why do you think he wants Danny?"

"He said something about taking Robin back to the forest," said Jamie.

"Now there's our first clue. I must find out more about this strange visitor. He could be a trouble maker."

"No, don't think about him. Find the team! You've got to bring all the players back from Legendworld before tonight. We've only got five hours before the match starts!"

CHAPTER THIRTEEN

THE MATCH

"Your Grandad was on the phone earlier," said Jamie's Dad as he switched on the electric kettle. "He says he'll pick you up at seven o'clock."

"I don't know if I'm going." Jamie pushed his empty plate across the table. "It's not worth it."

"You'll see Kev play."

"Dad, we won't win!"

"That's not good supporter talk. Nottingham Forest will need your cheering more tonight than any night. Come on, I'll make you some soup, but not tomato."

Jamie slumped on the settee in the lounge. The early evening news showed people laughing at a special celebrity wedding. The bride was cutting a tall, three - tiered cake. Jamie flicked the channels. Not even the cartoons could comfort him. The match was lost. Nothing was going to save them now.

"Watch your step, Jamie. I don't want to be diving in to save you. That river's pretty deep. Walk close to me," said Jamie's Grandad, as they walked along the riverbank to the Nottingham Forest Stadium. "Come on, less of that long face. They'll need all our support tonight. You've got to cheer loud enough for those folk in the Jumbo Jet to hear us."

"Jamie!" a voice called from behind them. "Lovely night, clear and warm. I think I could happily jump on that rowing boat and meander down the river."

Jamie looked round. It was Dierling.

"A good crowd tonight, inspite of the mishaps and team change," said Dierling, following Jamie through the turnstile into the ground. "I didn't expect so many people to turn out. The noise will be thunderous if Nottingham Forest win."

"Nottingham Forest supporters turn out rain or shine. I wouldn't expect there to be any less tonight," said Jamie's Grandad. "And it's not 'if' but 'when' we win."

"I'm sorry. Yes you're quite right," Dierling tried to apologise. "I do hope you both enjoy the match." He waved and walked ahead of them.

"Strange man," said Jamie's Grandad. "Do we know him?"

"He's the man from Save the Children," said Jamie. "He took me to the Club. He's called Mr. Dierling."

"Is he now? Well, here we are, then. This is our row - the last two seats. Do you want to sit on the outside or inside?" Jamie's Grandad offered Jamie the choice.

"I'll be all right at the end of the row," said Jamie. His Grandad shuffled along to the second seat and made himself comfortable. Jamie dropped the bag on the floor as he sat down.

"Watch you don't break that flask," said his Grandad. "And if you're not going to liven up I'll be wishing I'd left you at home. Look there's your friend Mr. Dierling along the row. He seems to be waving to you."

Jamie looked up. Dierling was waving and pointing to the pitch. A player emerged from the tunnel. It was Kevin.

"Grandad it's Kev." Jamie pulled his Grandad's sleeve.

"Kevin?" his Granddad looked up from reading the Match Programme. "It is Kevin. He's got a game with the Reserve Team. Good for him.

"No, he was supposed to be playing with the First Team," said Jamie.

"Why didn't he...?" But Jamie's Grandad's words were drowned by thunderous shouts and cheers.

"They're back! They're back!" shouted Jamie, joining in the celebrations as the whole of the first team ran onto the pitch. "He's done it! We're going to win!"

"This is incredible." His Grandad looked on in disbelief. "One minute they're gone and the next they're back. And there's Danny!"

There was a tannoy message across the stadium. "We are pleased to welcome back our First Team. The match will commence in ten minutes."

"So they're only showing us their faces," said Jamie's Grandad, as the players ran back down the tunnel. "This is a bit too much like magic to me. But I'm not complaining. We're going to the top, Jamie."

"Excuse me." Dierling was at Jamie's side. "I was wondering if I could have Jamie for ten minutes before the match. I've arranged for him to meet some of the players."

"Sounds all right to me," said Jamie's Grandad. "Is that okay with you?" He looked at Jamie. Jamie nodded. "Well, you go along with Mr Dierling. You know the seat number."

"I'll have him back in time," said Dierling.

"Tell them to sprinkle stardust on their boots. And bring me back an autograph, Jamie," his Grandad called after him.

"You found them all! You found the whole team in time for the match." Jamie grabbed Dierling's arm as they walked up the steps. "How did you do it?"

"Once I found the right file it was easy."

"Great, we're going to win now!"

"I'm afraid it is not that simple," said Dierling. "The game is not won yet."

"We will win! We will! They're all back."

"Jamie, I wish I could join in your optimism, but I'm afraid there's one person out there who could drown the team's chances for promotion."

"Who? Who is it?"

"Your friend in the bear suit."

"He can't take Danny! Why does he want Danny?"

"Jamie, the man in the bear suit is the legendary Friar Tuck. He believes that Danny is Robin Hood and he means to transport Danny back to Medieval Nottingham for an archery contest tomorrow."

"But Danny is Danny!" said Jamie.

"Maybe, I have no way of telling at the moment. So we will work from that belief. Either way, I am not happy with the Friar's manners. He is not a Legendworld Agent and he did not ask to borrow the devices."

"What's he going to do?"

"Cause a lot of trouble to everyone unless I work quickly. I believe he could have set a mechanism in the goal mouth."

"What do you mean?"

"He has stolen many devices from Legend world, including one which will activate the Trawl. He has probably set up the goal net so that once the ball hits it there will be a sudden burst of light and the Trawl will capture anyone within ten meters – including Danny."

"We can't let him take Danny!" said Jamie. "He belongs at the club."

"Is that the Friar?" Dierling pointed to a Sherwood Bear figure running onto the pitch.

"I don't know. The Club's got two bear costumes. That could be the mascot."

"Two bears, that makes it twice as difficult. We'd better move fast." Dierling took Jamie's arm.

"Where are we going?"

"To the changing rooms to find your cousin Kevin."

"Kev, what's he got to do with it? He doesn't know anything about Legendworld."

"Then, you'll have to tell him."

"Mr.Dierling, I don't think I can explain. Kev will never believe me. Anyway, how can he help?"

"Just trust me. He is the only one who can help now."

"I'm afraid you can't come down here." A steward blocked Dierling's path. "No one can go down the players' tunnel without authorisation."

"It's okay." Dierling held up a card from his pocket. "We'll be five minutes."

"Very well." The steward let them pass.

"Right, this could be tricky," said Dierling. "We need to get Kevin on his own. He'll probably be in the changing room."

"It's this way." Jamie rushed on ahead. At the door to the changing room he knocked then waited. A tall, dark haired player came to see what he wanted.

"Can I see Kev for a minute please? I'm his cousin."

"Kev, your cousin wants you!" the player called out.

"Jamie, is everything okay?" Kevin appeared at the door.

"Yes," said Jamie "Well, no, not really."

"I think I'd better explain." Dierling stepped forward.

"Who are you?" asked Kevin.

"He's from Legendworld," said Jamie.

"Jamie, what's this all about? I haven't got time for fairy stories. Is this man a newspaper reporter?"

"Please, just give me a few minutes of your time." Dierling caught Kevin's arm and his gaze. "Now, only a few minutes and all will be explained."

"Two minutes," said Kevin.

"Danny is in danger. I think someone is planning to capture him again. In fact I know."

"Then why don't you tell the police?" asked Kevin.

"Because it's not that simple," said Dierling.

"Mr. Dierling thinks Sherwood Bear is Friar Tuck," said Jamie, "and he's set up a device in the opposition's goal mouth so that when Danny scores he will be transported back to Medieval Nottingham!"

"Jamie, can I go now? I think you've been reading too many fairy stories." Kevin grew impatient.

"But you've got to believe me," Jamie pleaded.

"Kevin," Dierling spoke softly. "Can I just have a quiet word?" Kevin turned in the doorway.

"I will only keep you a minute," Dierling continued, staring into Kevin's eyes. Kevin said nothing but stood motionless, transfixed by Dierling's gaze.

"Now, Kevin, I would like you to do everything you can to prevent a goal being scored by your team in the first half of the game. The ball must not strike the back of the net."

Kevin was silent.

"Well, I wish you luck. We'll be cheering for you." Dierling's tone suddenly changed. He patted Kevin on the back.

"Thanks. Hey, you get Grandad to shout the loudest." Kevin ruffled Jamie's hair. It was as though nothing had happened. "I'll see you after the match." He disappeared into the changing room.

Jamie turned to Dierling, "What's going to happen? Kev doesn't believe us. Who's going to save Danny now?"

"I've done all I can. It is out of my hands until half time. We'll have to put our trust in your cousin."

"Safe and sound, returned." Dierling directed Jamie to his seat. Enjoy the game. Perhaps we'll meet again." He waved and walked back up the steps.

"Had a good time then? Three minutes and we're starting," said Jamie's Grandad. "Whose autograph did you get?"

"Oh sorry, I.. I forgot," said Jamie.

"Never mind. It must be all the excitement. The team look fit, wherever they've been. Young Kevin looks keen. Playing for the First Team. I wonder why he didn't tell me?"

"He wanted it to be a surprise," said Jamie.

"Well, it certainly was," said Grandad. "What a match to play in. It'll be tight. He'll have to keep his wits about him. Now they've got to hold them in this first half. We need at least one goal."

Jamie leant back in the seat.

"Hey can't rest there. You've got to be cheering them on! No shirking, you're a supporter! They're at the ready now."

The whistle blew. Centre pass. Danny was on the ball. The stadium was alight with cries of, "Come on you Reds!" Danny passed to another player. He was tackled. The ball went out of play. A throw in and Nottingham Forest had the ball again. Crossed to Kevin. Kevin raced ahead into the penalty box. The ball was in the air. Danny was there. He jumped, twisted and headed the ball straight towards the goal.

It hit the top bar and ricocheted back to Kevin's feet. The goalkeeper lay sprawled.

"Shoot! Shoot!" Grandad shouted as the crowd rose to their feet. Everyone held their breath as Kevin repositioned the ball and ... there was a huge groan.

Jamie couldn't see through the people in front. "What's happened? I thought Kev was going to score." He pulled on his Grandad's sleeve.

"So did everyone else in the stadium."

The supporters sat down again. "Clear it, clear the ball!" Jamie's Grandad shouted as the game livened. A Nottingham Forest player tackled, he had the ball. "Come on you Reds!" the crowd yelled as the player cut lose and tore through midfield.

"Pass! Pass now!" shouted Grandad as an opposition player ran in to tackle. The Forest player was brought down just outside the penalty area. The Referee ran up.

"We've go a free kick," said Grandad. "Now this is our chance."

The opposition crowded into an arc, waiting to run forward. The Forest player positioned the ball.
The kick was high. The ball soared over the opposition's wall of heads. Players ran into the goalmouth. The crowd rose.

"I can't see, I can't see!" shouted Jamie.

There was a roar, then a groan and Grandad sat down again.

"They're missing chances. Kevin again, I can't understand. He should have been on that ball. It was at his feet. It just needed a tap and it would have been in the goal. It was just as if his boots were laced together. I don't think we're going to get a ball in the back of that net before half time."

"Very disappointing," said Jamie's Grandad, as the whistle blew for half time. "They'll have to get their act together in the second half. I can see the 'whens' turning to 'ifs'. Come on, let's have some of this soup." He unscrewed the flask and warm vapours of mushroom soup rose, steaming his face. "Um – nice smell." He poured soup into one of the cups and passed it to Jamie. "There you are. Mind it's hot."

Jamie sat back with his soup, thinking. Kevin had worked well to keep the ball out of the net. Now everything would be all right in the second half. "We could still win, Grandad. I think we stand a good chance."

"Well, let's hope the players are as confident as you. How's the soup?"

"Fine." Jamie sipped on the lip of the cup, watching the men patting down the grass near the goal that Nottingham Forest would be kicking into when the second half began. Sherwood the Bear was leaping around, pretending to defend the goalmouth. The crowd was laughing and waving at his antics.

"Drink up, lad. Half time doesn't last forever. What's that bear up to? These mascots do anything to attract the crowd's attention. There's another one now! He's running to the goalmouth. Look, he's like a commando climbing up the net. He'll come a cropper."

Jamie watched the bear clinging to the white meshing. "There's your friend, Mr. Dierling. What's he doing on the pitch? He's chasing after the second Sherwood! This must be a publicity stunt for the charity."

Dierling dived for the bear's feet.

"It's rugby now!" Jamie's Grandad laughed as the two figures grappled and rolled across the pitch.
"A real drama feature, they're bringing in the heavy brigade now." Four stewards in yellow jackets ran onto the pitch and pulled the pair apart. The bear broke lose and ran to the sidelines. Dierling was led off the pitch.

"Come on, enough of the circus tricks," said Grandad. "Pass me your cup, Jamie. It'll be the second half soon. No goals so far, so we're still in with a chance."

Jamie looked out for Kevin as the players ran from the tunnel to the roar of the crowd.

"Now come on you Reds, let's see it happen. You can do it!" his Grandad shouted, waving his Nottingham Forest scarf. "Now show them what you're made of!"

The opposition had the ball – a cross. The player had a clear run.

"Tackle, tackle!" shouted Grandad. The fans rose from their seats as the ball entered the Forest goal area. Jamie peered between shoulders as the ball arrowed to the goal and flew straight into the hands of the keeper. There was a deep sigh of relief from the terraces and fans sat back in their seats.

The goalkeeper rolled the ball to the feet of one of his defenders. He kicked it to midfield. A Forest player flicked the ball to Danny.

"Danny!" Jamie shouted. "Danny!"

The player held the ball at his feet, teasing the opposition, pulling them into tackle then flicking the ball up and over their heads. Another Forest player caught it on his knee, levelled it to the ground and passed again. Danny was on the edge of the goalmouth now, well marked. An opposition player ran forward blocking.

"Pass! Pass!" shouted Grandad. The ball ricocheted off bodies and ran to ground. The keeper dashed forward and scooped it up. Players fell back, as he ran out to the edge of the penalty box and placed the ball to kick up field.

"So close," said Grandad. "They're playing well against stiff opposition. Don't need any distractions. Now concentrate!" The ball flew into the air. An opposition player ran in to take it. "Come on you Reds!" Jamie's Grandad shouted. "Sort them out. You can do it!"

"Only five minutes of the match left and no goals. We don't want a draw. We need to win this match," said Jamie's Grandad. "They've got to score a goal in the next few minutes. Take it up! Take it up!" he shouted.

Jamie sat on the edge of the seat. What was happening? Dierling had been so sure they would win. Forest had the ball again. The player swerved past a defender then passed to the left. The opposition raced in, kicking the ball over the touchline.

"Corner, it's a corner!" shouted Jamie. "This could be it."

"What's that bear doing again?" said Grandad. "He's behind the net! What's Sherwood doing out there now?"

Jamie watched the bear's antics. He had something in his hand and he was fixing it to the goal net. The referee blew the whistle and waved towards him.

"He won't go away," said Jamie.

"Well, he'll have to now. There's a steward running towards him." The game came to a stand still as Sherwood was rugby tackled and dragged from behind the goal.

"He's had a great day today," said Grandad. "We'll be into extra time because of that. Now, come on. Let's have this goal!"

The referee raised his hand to signal all was ready. But another figure, in a suit, was running onto the pitch. It was Dierling. Stewards lunged forward. The chase was on. Dierling swerved, darted, and wove his way between the army of yelling coats.

"What's he doing?" asked Grandad. "The fool!"

The players watched in amazement as the lean sprinter threaded between them, finally hurling himself into the goalmouth and grabbing the net. The stewards were upon him. He was lost under a sea of yellow. Then he appeared upright, in the grip of two stewards who escorted him to the side of the pitch. Jamie could see that he had something in his hand.

"I've never seen a game like it," said Grandad. "That was your Mr. Dierling again. Was that a charity run?" The crowd applauded at the scene, but were eager for the match to restart.

"Right, this is it," said Grandad. "Come on!"

The referee signalled. The player positioned the ball. All heads turned to the corner. The fans were up, straining to see the action. The ball was in the air. Kevin ran forward to take it on his chest. It bounced to the ground before his feet. The opposition raced into tackle. Kevin flicked the ball into the air. Heads rose, butting the air. Danny was there. He jumped high above the barrage of bodies. Twisting and lunging, he drove the ball into the back of the net.

The Stadium was alight. Jamie struggled to see the pitch, as fans waved and cheered. "We're going to the top, to the top!" rang out from all around. The referee blew the full time whistle. Scarves were thrown high and the stadium roared with applause.

"Grandad, we've won!" shouted Jamie.

"We've done it!" Jamie's Grandad squeezed his slim shoulders. "I told you nothing could stop them. Premiership, European cup. The sky's the limit! They've come through like real heroes!" He ruffled Jamie's hair. "Now we can really celebrate. Come on you Reds!"

**The voices and laughter faded into the distance
as the river flowed slowly beneath
the old Trent Bridge,
a carnival of lights reflected in the waters beneath.**

**Silhouetted against the night sky,
the great white stadium towered above.
Its seats still ringing with the cheers and applause,
saluting the team
that had made it**

TO THE TOP

Other books in the same series:

THE DRAGON IN CLEETHORPES

TROLL RELEASE

BLACKPOOL PHOENIX

Visit legendworld.co.uk to find out more.